Katy and Jamini Make It Rain

Story by Pamela Rushby

Illustrations by Alessia Trunfio

Contents

Chapter 1

A New Family in Town

Katy and her mum lived in a small country town. The town was surrounded by farms, and most of them grew … watermelons! The farmers were proud to say their farms produced a quarter of all the watermelons grown in the whole country.

A new family had come to live in the town: Mr and Mrs Kapur, their grown-up son, Adesh, and their daughter, Jamini. They had opened a shop, and Mr and Mrs Kapur and Adesh worked in it. Katy – and everyone else in town – had been to look at the shop. It was fascinating! It seemed to sell *everything*.

Katy had talked to Jamini when she and her mum visited the shop. Katy liked Jamini at once.

"You'll be coming to our school, won't you?" Katy said. "Will you be in my class? We must be the same age."

Jamini smiled back. "I hope I'll be in your class," she said. "That would be good."

On Saturday morning, there was a drum circle in the park. Katy loved going to drum circle. It had been started by Harry, one of the older boys at school. People got together in the park, brought their drums or percussion instruments and played together, just for fun. Katy had a hand drum, called a djembe. As she put it into her mum's car, she wondered whether Jamini would like to join the drum circle.

"Why don't I ask Jamini if she wants to come?" Katy said to her mum. "Could we call in at the shop on the way to the park?"

On the way, Katy and Mum passed Mr Chen, the town's mayor. He was busy putting up some notices about the town's watermelon festival, which was going to take place soon. It was held every year at this time, when it was hot and all the watermelons had ripened. Katy and Mum could see that Mr Chen was on his way to drum circle, too. He had a trolley with his big bass drum on it.

"I'd forgotten it was nearly festival time," said Mum. "The rains are late this year. I always remember it must be nearly festival time when the rains start."

"And it always rains at festival time," agreed Katy. "Everyone gets soaked – but we have a great time anyway! It's all part of the fun. I hope the rains come soon."

Chapter 2

Waiting for Rain

Mum and Katy pulled up outside the Kapurs' shop and went inside. "Hello, Mr Kapur," Katy said. "I came to ask Jamini if she'd like to come to drum circle with me today. Lots of kids from school are in it."

"I'd like to, but I haven't got a drum," Jamini replied.

"You don't need one. You can borrow one, or there'll be spare maracas and shakers there."

Mr Kapur looked pleased. "You should go, Jamini. You'll meet other kids from your new school there. Katy will look after you."

Mrs Kapur was talking to Katy's mum. "I'm worried," Mrs Kapur said. "Look at this big order of gumboots that's just arrived! I was told it always rains here at this time of year, so I ordered lots of gumboots. But look at the weather! No rain at all! I'll never sell all these!"

Katy had an idea. "Maybe you could have a stall at the watermelon festival," she suggested.

"But why would people want to buy gumboots at the festival?" Mrs Kapur asked.

"Because it always rains for the watermelon festival," said Katy. "Everyone gets wet. It's a lot of fun."

"A stall would be worth a try," said Adesh. "If Katy's sure it'll rain."

"It always does!" Katy said.

When Katy's mum dropped Katy and Jamini off at the park, they walked across to the drum circle. "This is my djembe," Katy told Jamini. "It's a type of drum that comes from West Africa. Some people have drums from the Caribbean or India, and some have shakers or bells."

But Jamini was looking at a tall object standing in the park. It was triangular and made of metal.

"What's that?" she asked. "Is it a statue?"

"Oh, that," said Katy. "It's an old rainmaker. It was used here more than a hundred years ago, in experiments to try to make it rain when there was a drought."

"How did it work?" asked Jamini.

"The farmers used it to fire explosives into the sky," said Katy. "I think they hoped the vibrations and noise would make it rain."

"Did it work?" asked Jamini.

"Not really. It only rained a few drops, so they never bothered using the rainmaker again. But it was left here in the park."

"Noise to make rain?" Jamini said. "That's interesting."

"Hi, Katy!" called Harry. "And you've brought Jamini! That's great! Come and join in, we're all ready to go. And guess what? We've been asked to perform at the festival!"

The drum circle began. **Boom! Boom!** went Mr Chen's bass drum. **Thumpa-thumpa-thumpa** went the hand drums. **Rattle-rattle** went the percussion instruments.

Everyone had a good time, and Jamini said she'd like to come again. "I'll see if Mum or Dad can get me a drum!" she said.

Chapter 3

Festival Day

Soon, the day of the festival arrived. It still hadn't rained. The Kapurs set up their gumboot stall in the park, beside lots of other stalls.

"It doesn't look like it'll ever rain," said Mrs Kapur, in a worried voice. "The sky is blue. The sun is shining. People are looking at our gumboots and laughing!"

The festival began. There was a parade through the town with bands, people marching and floats with watermelons on them. The parade ended at the park.

"The farmers save the watermelons that aren't quite perfect for the festival," Katy told Jamini. "So we have lots we can use for the competitions and games. Let's go and see everything!"

First, Katy and Jamini watched some little kids get their faces painted. They could be anything they wanted to be – as long as it was a watermelon! Then, the girls watched watermelon-throwing competitions and races where the competitors had to carry watermelons. They ate watermelon slices and drank watermelon juice. There was watermelon skiing, where people put their feet in hollowed-out watermelons and were towed along a course that was slippery with soap and watermelon pulp. There was even a poetry competition, for a poem to a watermelon.

What there *wasn't*, was rain.

Katy was getting worried. She would feel terrible if the Kapurs could not sell their gumboots. The stall had been her idea. She sat down to think about it on the grass. Jamini sat down beside her.

Harry saw them and walked over. "The drum circle is going to perform soon," he said. "Are you coming?"

"I don't know," said Katy.

Harry sat down. "What's the matter?" he asked.

Katy took a deep breath and told him about the Kapurs' gumboot stall. "And I said it would rain, like it always does!" she finished sadly.

"Hmm," said Harry. He looked up at the sky. There were just a few clouds, far away. "Maybe it'll rain soon."

Jamini had been thinking. "If people a hundred years ago thought that vibrations and noise from a rainmaker might make it rain, could a really, really loud noise, like from a drum circle, make it rain?" she asked.

"I don't know if that would work," Katy said. "The rainmaker wasn't very good at making rain."

"It can't hurt to try," said Harry. He looked up at the sky again and smiled to himself. "We'll give it a go."

Chapter 4

Signs of Storms

Katy and Jamini joined the drum circle. Harry asked everyone to play as loudly as they could. **BOOM! BOOM! BOOM!** went Mr Chen's bass drum. **THUMPA-THUMPA-THUMPA** went the hand drums. **RATTLE, CRASH!** went the percussion instruments. The drum circle was amazing! The whole park vibrated with their drumming. Everyone in the crowd clapped and cheered.

And suddenly, the sun dimmed. The clouds grew bigger and blacker, and came racing across the sky. And then – it rained. It poured. It teemed!

Everyone rushed to get under cover. The storm passed quickly, and the sun came out again. But the park was now covered in mud, pools of water and watermelon pulp. People were up to their ankles in it. And the first place they went to was the Kapurs' gumboot stall! The gumboots were sold out in no time.

Katy and Jamini went to talk to Harry. "Did our drum circle really make it rain?" they asked.

Harry laughed. "Well …" he said. "When you've lived on a watermelon farm as long as I have, you learn the signs that tell you a storm is coming."

"Signs? What signs?" Katy and Jamini wanted to know.

"Well, for one thing, my dogs get nervous," Harry said. "They don't like storms. They won't lie down, and they pace around the house looking anxious. And last night, the frogs in our dam were croaking a lot louder than they usually do. And then, I can kind of smell it – there's more ozone in the air when rain's coming. It smells sharp and fresh." He grinned at them. "But maybe it was our drumming. You never know."

Jamini's family had sold out of gumboots. Adesh went off to practise a dance for the talent competition.

Mrs Kapur went to read her poem to a watermelon in the poetry competition.

And Mr Kapur, who was very big and strong, won the Melon Ironman competition – carrying a giant watermelon first across the finish line.

At the end of the day, there was a bonfire and barbecue. Katy, her mum and the Kapurs went to buy some dinner, and to wait for Adesh to perform his dance in the talent competition.

"Do you like our watermelon festival?" Katy asked the Kapurs.

Mr and Mrs Kapur laughed. "It's a lot of fun," Mr Kapur said.

"And we've sold a lot of gumboots," said Mrs Kapur. "I hope we do as well next year! Do you think it will rain next year, Katy?"

Katy and Jamini looked at each other. "I'm not sure," Katy said. "But we know the signs to watch for now!"

"And we'll have our drums, just in case," said Jamini.